LISTEN GIRL!

LISTEN GIRL!

Krishna Sobti

translated by

SHIVANATH

First published by Katha in 2002

KATHA
A-3 Sarvodaya Enclave
Sri Aurobindo Marg
New Delhi 110 017
Phone: 652 4350, 652 4511
Fax: 651 4373
E-mail: editors@katha.org
Internet address: http://www.katha.org

KATHA is a registered nonprofit society devoted to enhancing the pleasures of reading. KATHA VILASAM is its story research and resource centre.

Cover Design: Geeta Dharmarajan
Cover Painting: Prokash Karmakar
Courtesy: Delhi Art Gallery

Editor: Geeta Dharmarajan
In-house editors: Shoma Choudhury, Gita Rajan

Typeset in 9 on 15.5pt Bookman by Sandeep Kumar at Katha and Printed at Usha Offset, New Delhi

ISBN 81-87649-21-6

2 4 6 8 10 9 7 5 3 1

CONTENTS

on writing *Ai ladki*

KRISHNA SOBTI

Memory is a rare gift. Whatever you remember of an intense moving experience becomes a part of your personal text. Writers like me touch the pen, with a prayer to God – Bless me with ears that hear flowers and sunshine, moonlight. Give me sight that I can see a sigh of joy, the anguish of sorrow.

When my mother was in the intensive care unit, I remember hearing her repeat the words, "The light will keep burning." Those lines haunted me for many days and nights and came to be *Ai ladki*, this novel. But strangely, the words that started the story are not in it.

My mother was called Durga Devi. Her mortal remains were consigned to the fire with the chanting of mantras and her last rites were performed according to family tradition. And in her room back at home, an earthen lamp burnt day and night, steadily, as if saying that the body perishes, not the soul. For the soul has neither birth nor death.

Nights, I, unable to sleep, would stand in the doorway of her room, staring at the flickering flame of the diya. My mind empty, the bed and bedside cabinet forlorn.

On the fourth day after the havan, I took the morning flight to Srinagar. My mother's illness had been long, I was exhausted. And for long at Pehalgam, I could not, would not, listen to the rhythmic roar of the Liddar, nor notice the snowcapped mountains. I felt I was not me, there was another living within.

One afternoon as I woke up from a nap, I looked at the watch, laced my shoes in a hurry and ran to the bus stop. That morning, the caretaker of the cottage had informed me, with his usual gentleness, if I would like something since he was off to Srinagar, I had shaken my head. As usual too. What could I need?

I had thought in the morning I did not need anything. And now I wanted to give him a list of stuff I needed – pen, pencil, paper ... wondering why on earth I had thought in the morning that I didn't need a thing.

I spotted him standing near the bus, looking surprised at seeing me rushing up to him, saying, But I had asked you in the morning, behan. You could have saved yourself all this trouble if only ...

He boarded the bus. I waved, he waved back. I felt warm and light and began walking towards Pehalgam bazaar.

And then it was that I saw a herd of horses near the river bank. My mother's image flashed unbidden through my mind. All through her sickness, she had talked horses, she who was always in natural command when she rode those horses of hers. Lying in the bed she thought horses.

No, I must divert my mind from the drama of death I thought, as, again unbidden, another day came stealing into my mind. The family doctor had told her lightly —

Ma-ji, take things easy, everyday is a blessing, eat whatever you desire.

She had smiled.

Next morning when I brought her breakfast she looked hard at me and said, My horse is gone. What would I do with the saddle?

I avoided looking at her.

Late in the evening she asked me for something hot to drink.

As I brought her a cup of milk she gave me a piercing look and said,

Daughter, I wanted to scale the mountains – but where was the time? Your father's household consumed every moment. Do you understand?

She looked long and hard at me. Then she said,

No you don't – you stand outside this. Ai ladki, the family takes away all one has ...

After this she would not call me by my name, she simply said Ai ladki, Hey girl. Was she creating a distance between the dying and the living?

I started walking fast. Suddenly I spotted a high yellow flag fluttering in the air, a gurudwara, a shrine of my mother's faith. I decided to go in. A turbaned priest was reciting verses from the Adi Granth, the scripture of my mother's faith. I quietly sat in a corner, my eyes closed. When I at last opened them, it felt as if I had had a final message from my mother. Look at the mountains, the river heights, and the green. You are in Kashmir. My death is not the end of the world for you. Little did I know this was something I could not shake off easily. I was bound so intensely to that past that I just had to touch it again.

Me, my mother's daughter. And she her daughter's mother. On my way back I bought cherries – red and fresh – and felt happy.

That evening I sat a long while in the veranda, completely at peace with myself. The evening sky was painted raingrey, with threatening fat clouds that flashed resounding thunder and brilliant lightning. I watched the falling rain till late in the night, hearing only the silences within me.

It was much later that I opened all the windows in my room and switched on my table lamp. As I picked up my pen I heard my mother say,

Ai ladki ...

Instinctively I knew: Here were the key words. They came quietly to move into my fingers. I did not have the slightest idea I was going to create a symbol of deep personal value with those very ordinary words, Ai ladki. As I wrote I knew with ever growing confidence that I could provide the spiritual framework to accommodate the deep intimacy of those words, their comforting presence inside every bit of me. I knew I would create an abiding togetherness between a dying woman and her daughter, the fading and failing interior, the unsaid words, the silences that record more than words that last her statement, a text of the undying human spirit.

There were two different generations, two very different times, two almost diametrically opposite identities. One a woman, a mother entrenched in her home and family. And the other a single individual outside the family fold. A new woman.

Between the initial bits-and-pieces memory and the concrete realization of a creative idea, much goes on. But when the writing happens, all the complexity of a thinking mind goes in amazing tandem with an involvement that can only be called emotional detachment. That spark is not skill or style or language; it is of the mind, mysterious, magical. We all have different ways of touching reality and distilling the centre of our vision. For me it is an image, powerful and lingering, a too-deep-to-understand artistic capacity, a strong intellectual capability touched by unknown inner energies. A magical combination indeed to weave the human narrative!

In *Ai Ladki* I know what I have done. I've mixed the different elements of life, the words mingling with the very age and body of time, the human drama of the last statement of a dying woman with the stubborn resilience of the younger woman. It was so powerful that I needed great restraint and merciless accuracy. To not overdo it all.

No, no one is exempt from literary failings. But I believe what's important is honesty and intellectual integrity, an inner dimension to visualize a touch, a sensation, a dream, a challenge. And finally, a sudden madness, a leap into space, to create a thing vibrant and alive.

This piece first appeared in the Literary Review page of *The Hindu*, on 3 Feburary 2002. It has been slightly modified for this volume.

Ai Ladki was first published in Hindi in1991.

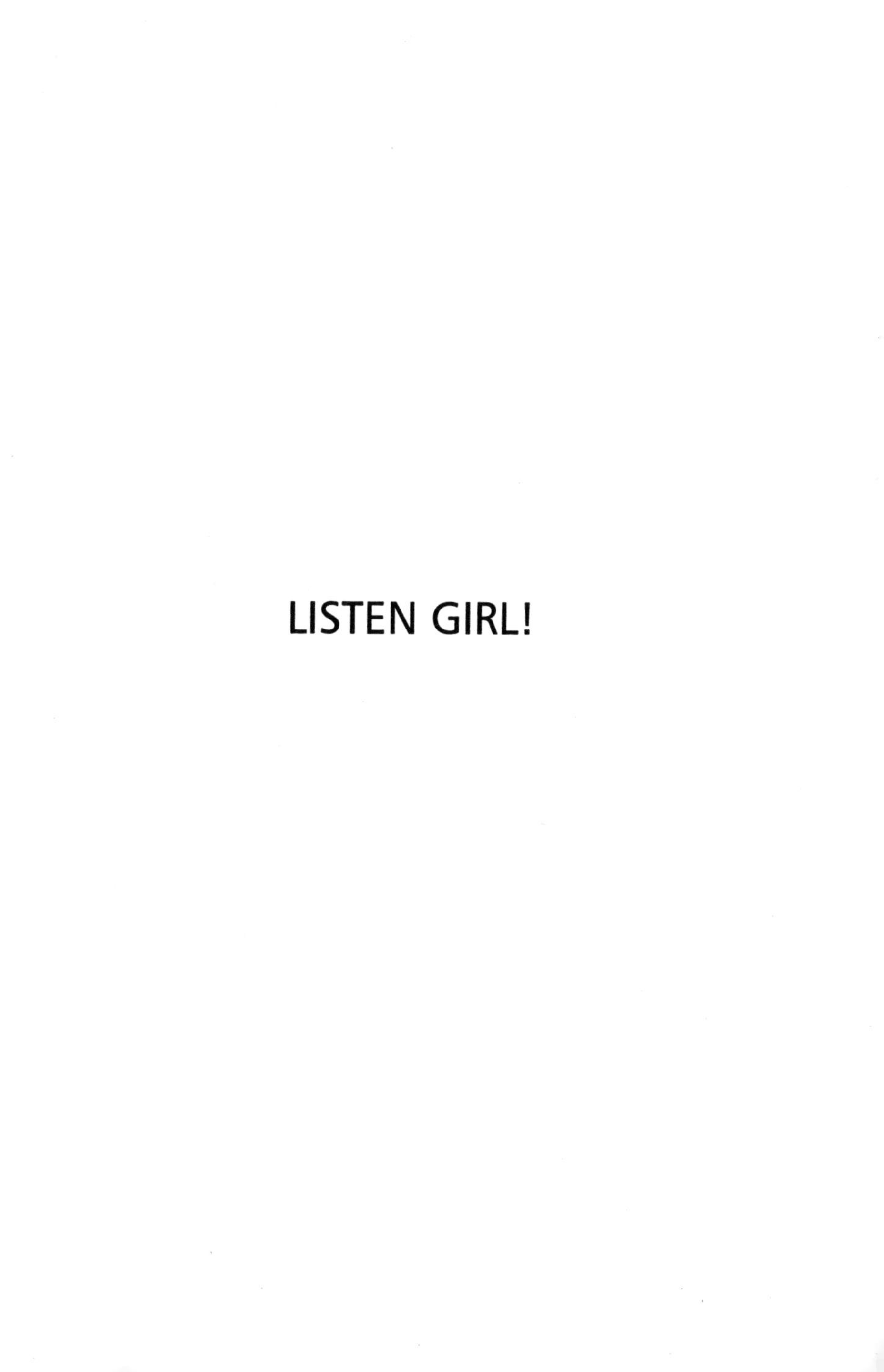
LISTEN GIRL!

– You girl! Why have you kept it so dark in here? Stinging on electricity, are you? Have we actually come down to this now?

– Ammi, every single light in the house is on. Even the table lamp.

– So it's I who calls light darkness, hahn? No ladki, I haven't taken leave of my senses, no not yet. But if *you* people want to see silver snakes in the dark, who can stop you?

Now, why are you so silent?

Tongue refusing to budge or what?

On top of that, this Susan's eyes too don't speak ...

Tell me, what are you people afraid of?

– Ammi, relax. Aren't you suffering enough?

– Yes, but don't you forget one thing: I haven't let that illness run amuck inside me, or it would've sucked me dry by now.

Now what have I said that you've clammed up like a little blue bird?

– Am-*mi!*

– Listen child, the chain-latch on my door is down. Barely one knock and I'm out. But I'm not one to give in to disease and illness, man's worst enemies. They shatter the links between body and mind, robbing the body even of its own, accustomed smell ...

These damn medicines. They enter the blood and dry the body to a lifeless reed and ...

What's got into my head child, that I ...

Oh this room reeks of illness! And the way things once were has disappeared for ever, gone ...

– Ammi, can I burn some dhoop?

– Have you taken leave of your senses, child? This is a sick woman's room, not a puja room ...

You may put some roses in the vase if you so please. Their smell will stay. Those big gorgeous roses ... Where did I see them now, where, where ...

A-i ladki, I can't think ... I fear my brain's all fossilized!

– Ammu, don't worry so. Flowers are everywhere. It's not necessary to remember each and every place you saw them in.

– It's the medicines. They play havoc inside me, blindfolding thoughts. But tell me ladki, what has come over you? Your voice that I remember, where has its sweetness gone, child, its mellowness?

– Ammu, would you like to drink something cold?

– There, you've gone and changed the topic! Chalo, give me something, anything that comes from the generosity of your heart!

Child listen to me. Our roles have reversed. You my daughter have now become my mother and I ...

Let it be, let it be ...

You know that patient of mine ...

– Who, Ammi?

– That doctor of mine!

Ammi chuckles.

– I understand my illness, but does he? The soul has to find one way or another to leave the body, no?

Ammu dozes off.

The telephone rings. Ammu, startled.

– Who called?

– It was Chacha.

– Be specific, ladki. Your uncle or mine?

– Chhoté Chacha called.

– Oh that younger brother-in-law of mine, na? You should've put him on to me. But then, he's more your uncle than my brother-in-law these days. You talk about him as if he's unrelated to me. Remember I'm still alive and alert.

– Chacha asked about your health.

– I hope you are not making a song and dance about my illness to everybody.

When I came here as a bride, he was very young. Maybe

four or five years old. Some mischievous girl placed him in my lap and ...

– Were you embarrassed?

– I was the bride, he a mere child, my little devar! Bas. I fondled and kissed him. It was a charmed moment. All the girls and women around me collapsed with laughter. I remember that day. They filled my lap with gifts ... coconuts, almonds, dried dates ...

Actually, it's enough if, about once a week, you make all the right noises about an old person's health. That'll do.

As for me ...

I'm going to be around anyway, ladki. Haven't I worked hard to toughen this body of mine? It'll take its own sweet time to waste away.

Are you listening child?

– Ji.

– Ladki, there is no place for old people, not in anyone's heart not in anyone's house, and here I am, occupying an entire room.

After I'm gone, spread a carpet here and play your music.

– *Ammu*, why do you have to say such things?

– No need at all. Just flapping my wings that's all.

Ladki. You've looked after me in my last days, made it comfortable. As your mother, I suckled you and you, my own little one, you delighted in my milk. But our relationship isn't just one of flesh and blood, is it? It's of the soul, right? Isn't it, all connected, intertwined ...

Arri? I don't know why your life's turned out to be so different.

Why ... Where are you going? Why have you got up?

Sit with me for a while.

Don't go, ri.

Ammu, begins to doze.

After a short nap.

– I fell asleep and your nani's face kept flickering before my eyes. How many years since I dreamt of my mother. That same olive green salwar kameez and, peeping through her odhni, her breasts.

Ammu smiles slightly.

– I knew I was dreaming, yet there was that question inside me: Why am I not still suckling at Ma's breast?

I was still a baby when my sister was born. And I'd watch entranced whenever Ma breastfed her, staring, staring till one day Ma asked –

Kyun ri, why do you stare so? When you were a baby, you too lay in my lap and sucked my milk.

And I said –

Yes Ma, but just once more Ma?

Ma didn't get annoyed. She touched my chin and said –

Muniya, once you stop drinking your mother's milk, you stop. Can't turn that clock back. Now it's your little sister's turn. Don't be greedy. That's the first law of nature. You'll understand it all by and by ...

It seems as if it was only the other day, Ladki, I saw Ma sit breastfeeding my little sister. When you have a child at your breast, all the three worlds seem steeped in the sweetest, most heavenly syrup!

The mother eats and eats ... and the child takes it all!

Suddenly glaring at her daughter.

– What do you know of this miracle? Books can't tell the first thing about it. And staring at the wall won't bring images onto it. If that were so, what all you wouldn't have created by now!

Na, na ladki, apples can't grow on semal trees.

The daughter rises abruptly from the chair.

– Listen, don't go. I don't want to upset you. Surely friends can at times talk like this?

– I neither talk like this nor listen to such talk ...

– How can you? It is all empty inside. Barren. I can't see anything else.

Can you?

The daughter leaves the room abruptly.

Ammi, to herself.

– We humans! First we make things. Then we start accumulating. This is mine. This too is mine. Then in time the closed fist opens. And everything begins to just slip away. But look here!, this body is a mere garment. Wear it and you're in this world. Take it off and you're in another world, away from your own!

Lok-Parlok! Par-lok. A world of others. Not one which is your own, not one ...

Not one ...

Who knows how many stars there are in this universe.

One each for the living. One each for the dead. And some for people like me, sick people ...

Susan, listen to my words. Old age robs one of all dignity. Awful, to whosoever whensoever it comes.

Whispering to herself.

– Operations, medicines, injections, oxygen. Doctors dig and mine the whole body, jab hundreds of needles, examining, examining. When they are done, all that's left is the voice. And you're left staring, glaring at the ceiling or gaping at the past with eyes closed tightly shut.

O I think I'm down inside a dungeon. Ancient shadows rise before my eyes only to get lost before them forever ...

But then, why fear the past? Isn't it mere smoke that precedes fire. This body is made to last a hundred years.

If only I hadn't broken my leg by falling, I'd have been quite fine.

Susan gives her the medicine and turns down the light.

– Ammiji, sleep for a while.

– Susan, you have served me well, how can I repay you? At times I feel so guilty.

Seeing her daughter peering into the room.

– Come, ladki, sit with me for a while. Child, I feel I'm walking through bushes and brambles. Remember those thorny bushes on the hillsides? They've sprung up all over my head.

– Ammi. This is only because of those sleeping pills.

– Ladki. Dry leaves rain inside me, child, a dry, dry rain of leaves, with not a drop of wetness to it.

Listen girl. In the beginning parents hold infant fists and teach their children to walk. Then they grow old and become children of their children.

I understand your burden. I must have tired you out.

Why don't you go away for a few days?

– Not tired, Ammu, I just feel trapped all the time ...
Cornered.

– I know you well, child. You're afraid of my illness.
Sorrow or happiness, neither suits you.

Now pray for an early release for your mother.

– Ammi, why must you think like that? You're strong.
Everything will be just fine. Your courage will see you through this. Why, even the doctors admire your will power!

– You're right. As a child, I could fly, higher and higher, as if I had the power somewhere inside me. I was so very strong.

We all have a fire within us. The body draws its energy from it. But ladki, both my doctors are determined to extinguish it.

After sleeping for a while.

– You people have seen me only in my old age. Not as that girl who was about to be your mother. How long ago was that, in another eon, hahn, a different age ...

The sky is neverending, so too the earth. Only the race that we bipeds contest comes to an end.

Suddenly, self-conscious.

– Ladki, am I blabbering? Stop me if I am.

The daughter gets up from the chair.

Please ... Don't go yet. Stay a while longer. What do you have in that other room? If there's something there, tell me now. I want to know.
– Nothing Ammi, there's absolutely nothing there.

Ammu, talking to herself –

– Head, forehead, face. Eyes, nose, ears. Cheeks, hands, feet and waist. What all has the creator created! And inside is a programmed clock; wound to the last second. Not a breath more, nor a breath less ...

Those who build houses on earth have to move out of them one day.
– Ammu, let's talk about something else.
– Listen girl, can you not think of anything else but yourself! Why are you so annoyed with someone who will soon be out of your whole life?

Irritation, all the time irritation!

The patient's down?

Let her be.

She calls?

Respond.

She asks for something?

Give.

– Ammu, you put me through very hard tests.
– No way ladki, I never test or judge anyone, not now, not ever. If I call out to you again and again, child, it is to draw strength from you.

Seeing you, I feel I am still alive. Alive and kicking.
– Ammi ... What's troubling you, Ammu?
– Ai ladki, nothing I can describe. Grief so intense that one has to experience it all alone.
– Mamu, is it paining too much?
– No, not that much. Just that all things from the past and future mesh and meld before my eyes ... Ladki, distract me. My mind is all addled and strange shadows from the netherworld roam this room day and night ...
– Ammu, shall we talk about the hills? Shall we start with Shimla?

Ammu softly.

– My first hill journey was only from Kalka to Shimla. That was the first place I went to after my marriage, my heart full of joy, excitement. I sat at the window of the narrow gauge train from Kalka, gazing out of the window. Hills flirting with one another, deep soaring trees. And golden flowers fluttering by like pennants.

Entreatingly.

– Ladki, will I ever see these roads again? Will you take me there?

– Why not? As soon as you feel better, we'll take off.

– You must be joking but chalo, it feels good to hear that.

– Ammu, what happened during that Kalka–Shimla trip?

– Your grandmother had got a food basket ready for the journey with lemons and oranges and pickles and churan and those tart aam-paapads. Every time the train emerged out of a tunnel, she would ask –

Bahu, are you feeling dizzy? Queasy?

I would say No, and go back to staring out of the window.

Your father didn't like my saying No. In a commanding tone, he said –

Reply properly. Are you sure you aren't feeling dizzy?

As your Dada sahab was with us I felt diffident about replying. Then I thought, Where's the harm in saying what I feel? And I blurted out–

When I have resolved that I will not feel dizzy, why would I feel dizzy?

Your father frowned –

These are mountain roads, one's resolve doesn't work here.

But Dada sahab smiled and quietly gestured to his son –

I'm very pleased with our daughter. She's done a lot of horse riding. She knows how to control horses. That gives her her confidence.

Your dada and dadi laughed, but your pitaji sat sullenly.

I don't know why something said so innocently cast a shadow between him and me for such a long time. Every once in a while, your pitaji would say in his grand voice –

Being accomplished means knowing a lot of things. Merely knowing how to ride horses won't do.

Ladki, a man must always be in control. His place is up there, not down here ...

If there's such a thing as rebirth, then in my next birth, I'd like to be born a man. I'll then know how a warrior on the move controls his women and the family. Don't laugh. I'm serious. Every woman knows and understands this.

After a brief nap.

– Oh? Is it chai-time again? Ladki why don't you have milk with some little something in it. That'll keep the exhaustion off.

– Ammu, you're feeling better, na?

– Yes child. I dozed off even while talking to you. Don't know where my thoughts went wandering.

I dreamt that I was walking through a thick fog, now up Jakhoo Hill, now down the slope to Tooti Kandi. I was alone but I could hear footsteps behind me. High-heeled shoes, chasing, chasing me.

These dreams!

It was only as I approached the tunnel near Summerhill that I realized that it was my own shoes that I was hearing. An old, much used pair that your father had got made by a Chinese shoemaker, soon after our marriage.

Cream coloured leather,

soft as silk,

the heels tall and slim but so light to walk in that you could reach Mashobra in the twinkling of an eye.

Ladki, I don't walk fast now, do I, ri? But there was a time when I used to walk very fast. Must have bragged about it. I'm paying for it now.

Ammu opens her eyes after a long silence.

– It has snowed heavily. The field next to the church is covered with snow. Why has the church clock stopped ticking? It has not struck the hours for a long time. Just see what time it is.

The daughter looks at her wristwatch.

– Four.

Ammi, once more on her journeys.

– We are about to reach Kalka. We have left Barog behind quite some time ago. The tea you get there is superb, impossible to match.

The daughter stares past the table lamp.

Ammu is feeling the bed with her hands.

– Where's my fur coat? I was wearing it, wasn't I? See if it's on the upper berth.

Search ri! It's my favourite coat. Your father had the fur specially bought, direct from a shepherd.

Found it?

– Ji, it was in your cupboard.

Ammu remains silent for a long time.

Then in a sudden sharp voice.

– You people are already misplacing my things. This is disgusting.

Susan, bring my spectacles from the cabinet.

Also my dentures.

Brush them clean and give them to me. Why didn't you think of this? It's your duty to the patient, isn't it? Ai ladki, see how careless she's become.

Where are my keys? They were in my purse. Get them, get them ...

So, are they there or not?

The daughter takes the purse from the cupboard and gives it to her mother.

Ammi rummages inside it and finds the bunch of keys. Then, as if remembering something.

– My gold coins were also in this purse. Where are my guineas?

– They are in the locker, Ammu. Don't worry.

In deep thought, Ammi looks around the room as if searching for something.

– Tell me something, ladki. I haven't seen your pitaji for many days. Where is he?

The daughter places her hand on her mother's head.

– Ammi, rest a while. Then we'll get down to making the morning tea.

Helpless, Ammi looks towards the door. Then in a feeble voice.

– Give me something to eat. My mouth is dry.

The daughter to Susan.

– Bring me the jar of dry fruits.

The daughter puts some dry currants in Ammu's mouth after removing their pips.

Ammi, chews this for some time. Then.

– The last fruit of the season, child. This is joy indeed, sheer joy.

Have you seen an almond tree, ladki? No? Oh-ho, but then, how could you have? Ladki, just that one pleasure is the springboard for many others.

No, you haven't found it, have you?

Dawn.

The daughter draws aside the door and window curtains to allow the light in. Ammi stares into space for a long while then, all of a sudden, in a shrill voice.

– So. Since when have you taken over this chore of mine? So you've pushed me aside finally and become Me. This is my responsibility. Always. To first draw the curtains, then close them.

Mine.

– Ammu, were you able to sleep at all?

– Yes, but only in the early part of the night.

Ladki, dawn is a great blessing. The one who sleeps through it, misses so much. They see neither the union of day and night nor their parting. When birds sing in the faint flush of daybreak, the entire creation reverberates with it. It is truly auspicious to be up at first light. But your family ... It is the sort which bathes at night. But I refused to imitate your family in this, ladki. You know me. I always bathe in the dark of early dawn. Then I'd walk around Jakhoo, even in softly falling snow. Your father always got up late. I'd give him tea on my return.

Ladki, in winter the monkey brigade would come chattering down from Jakhoo to stake their claim on the roads. Leaping here, there, everywhere! One morning they surrounded me. I had my stick of course but I stopped and said gently –

Na beta, na. Let Ma pass. Tomorrow I'll bring you some roasted gram.

Ladki, monkeys understand everything. They moved aside and let me pass.

– And the chané, Ammu?

– I took some along the next day.

Ladki, I can still see the church road and the large room of our Shimla house. When it snowed, there was always an angithi burning in the room, day and night.

Wonder where those days have gone!

– Susan, have you given Ammu a wash?

– What are you saying ladki! I'm not a piece of cloth to be washed and spread out to dry, am I? I have rinsed my mouth, had my face and hands washed and the bed sheets changed. I'm now all set for the daily addiction of dawn.

Chai!

The daughter places the tea tray on the table.

– Let's start with this. Carrot murabba.

Ammu, pleased.

– Just the preserve would have been enough. Why put cream on top of it.

You know, this is lack of training, that's what. You are always either overdoing things or doing nothing; it's either a flood or a drought, always.

Suddenly, with a frown.

– You aren't trying to pay off all your debts in this life itself, are you, so that all this family giving and taking comes to an end? You know how to act your part, yes pretend, pretend till the very end. Just remember that I don't care.

Your ma, ladki, has lost interest in everything except food and drink.

Susan adjusts the pillow, raises Ammi's head and gives her a cup of tea.

Ammu, holding the cup, excitedly.

– Drink tea, Live long! The slogan of the tea company seems to have been written for me. Thanks to tea, I'm still alive.

Delighting in the tea.

– Subtract the first eighteen years of my life, I drank milk till then, and multiply the rest at the rate of four cups a day and you'll know how many cups of tea this woman has drunk.

She laughs.

– Who knows how many more cups are destined for me.

The daughter places her empty cup on the table.

– Shall I play your favourite record, Ammu?
– Yes, but first one more cup of tea! Morning tea is no less than music. Water, at first boil, the cup, nicely warmed, and the tea leaves in the kettle, fresh and strong, mmm ... what sweeter music!

Susan laughs.

– Ammiji, tea companies should have heaped you with prizes!
– Oh, but they did! I have tins and tins of Lipton Green. All got in exchange for coupons that I collected at exhibitions. Ladki, many things have changed in my kitchen, but the tea's always Lipton Green.

Listen children. Chai. It's life's gift to the living. Drink. As long as there's life, never ever stop. No matter what, your glass is destined to lie unclaimed after that.

The daughter stops pouring the tea.

– Na-na, don't stop. It's wrong to leave a cup half-filled. Even a cup has its dignity. It offers others a drink but can't quench its own thirst. Just imagine. Did its creator know what he had wrought? No ladki, a cup is made to be picked up, lifted to the lips, sipped, and drunk. Drink as long as you can.

The daughter bursts out laughing.

– Ammu, once more?

Ammi first looks surprised, then says angrily.

– Once more? What? Are you mocking me? Tormenting a sick old woman. This is really bad.
– But Ammi, I didn't mean to hurt you.
– Hmm ... It is me who thinks useless thoughts, yes? I sit on the seashore counting waves, right? Don't provoke me into saying things I'd rather not.
– Ammu, I didn't mean a thing, honest. I'm sorry if I hurt you.
– Don't forget that you're talking to your mother, ladki, not distributing toffees over the telephone. A smile here, a joke there, a flirting glance. Just look at yourself! Who are you? Tell me! People your age are grandmothers. And you? You think you are still in first bloom.

The daughter keeps her eyes glued to the wall opposite.

– I know exactly what you are waiting for. Your mother dead, and you free. Liberated. And then pray, whom will you boss around? Who do you have in the queue behind you? You! Neither a mother nor a grandmother. You are nothing, ladki, nothing. Nothing more than a vegetable. A blade of grass. A shard of straw! Do you even understand what I am saying?

The daughter, screaming.

– Enough Ammi.
– Why, what have I said? Only what everyone knows. This can't be said in any other way.

The daughter gets up from the chair.

– Where are you going?
– I'll get you some fresh tea. Want some cardamom in it?
– For me you add cardamom to milk. Never to tea.

Susan picks up the tray.

– No, no, let it be. I know my daughter. She'll get me milk. Not tea. First she'll heat it well. Then she will work it into a froth. She'll add some almonds next. So many that their fragrance will be suppressed. Susan, are you listening? Her eyes have no control over her hands. Hands acquire habits only when one has a family. That exquisite balance comes by itself.

As for her, she spends what she gets. The colour of respect is something else altogether! Neither too much, nor too little. Managing a household teaches one the virtue of measure. Add a handful where a handful is needed, a pinch where a pinch is needed. But she has no sense of proportion. She is always at a loss ... God knows why. She has three or four servants, yet, I'm tired, she says. She's made work even of my illness. Never in my life have I ever seen her sleep at night. No friend, no mate. She spends her time with books.

And on top of it, look at her attitude so proud to be alone.

Seeing Susan smile.

– What are you listening to? Eavesdropper you! I'm talking to myself on the telephone.

The daughter comes in with milk.

– Ammu, do you want to call someone? Which number should I dial?
– How can you dial my number? You want to know the secrets I have hidden behind the seven veils? Ladki, are you keeping a watch on me? That's not good.
– Ammu, just take a sip and tell me if it's all right. Sugar's fine?
– Yes. You have already tasted it. Raisins, cardamom and cinnamon. And five almonds.
– How did you know that?
– When you were grinding them, my ears were watching. I'm in vanaprastha, the last stage of a man's life. Ears watch and eyes listen. Old age has but empty footsteps to choose from ...

Ladki, tell me, if I pick up one end of the thread, the other disappears. What does a fractured hip have to do with memory?
– No, Ammu. You're more alert and observant than I am. Ask the doctor what he thinks of his patient.

– I know the doctors only too well. Don't you dare phone him to discuss me. He'll immediately tell you that your mother is out of her mind and will prescribe one more medicine.

Both burst into laughter.

– Ladki, when a patient has been ill for a long time you can diagnose anything. Really speaking, old age itself is the culprit. Of course there are lots more diseases in Doctor sahab's book. Prescriptions follow prescriptions. No clout in his medicines, nor in our fees. But I must admit that my doctors work hard. It's my body's that's given up.

After all ...

– Ammu, try to take your mind off all this for a while.

– You're right, but tell me what can I do? I'm plagued by the enemy. I can only moan, cry. The body lies bruised ...

Ladki, you can't hear the clink of bangles near this bed. Or the cry of a new born. What doctors have spent on the paraphernalia here would have been enough to bring up a child. Ladki, thinking does not make a baby! It's hard work, a mother's blood and sweat.

Long silence.

– The human race challenges death by giving birth to children. Arri, you who ride a buffalo like the god of

death, you'll destroy, but we'll create anew by the grace of the sun. Yes ladki, the Sun is the grand hero of the universe. Other planets are nowhere near.
– Ammu, they say Kunti had a son from the sun.
– No. If the sun had covered Kunti, life would've been annihilated. The fact is that every male in this world draws his strength from the sun. By the sun's grace is he invigorated, his passions aroused.
– And the woman ...?
– She favours the Earth. She is the supreme energy. She surrounds the male from all sides, drawing him within her folds.

Susan, what are you doing? Don't fiddle with the light switches. I don't like darkness. I'm not going to sleep yet.

Ammu closes her eyes. Then she suddenly opens them and stares at her daughter.

– What is it, Ammu?
– Ladki, I think white ants are eating into you. They must have eaten you hollow by now.

Tell me why didn't you too leave me and go away. You kept drawing nourishment from these your roots. What did you desire? Tell me. Don't be quiet.

Say something.

Tell me.

– *Ammu!*

– I was thrust on you, right? Ladki if you knew that, why didn't you snatch this snake from around your neck and throw it away? Nobody tied your hands, did they?

Listen child. No one in this world can steal your desires. Don't you ever hold me responsible for this. Not now, not in the future.

Exhausted, Ammu closes her eyes.

Susan gives Ammi some glucose.

Ammi feels better. Seeing her daughter seated in the chair, she looks pleased.

– Listen ladki, when I was a little girl, I used to sit in the courtyard and stare at the trees. Many a times, my grandfather must've seen me like this. One day he sat me by his side and said –

What do you stare at like that? They are not even fruit bearing trees.

I said –

Dadaji, I look at the dance of the trees. In the sun's rays, the leaves seem to be now silver now green. How beautiful they are in the breeze.

Dadaji was delighted when he heard that. For a long time then we sat there, he caressing my head. Again and again.

How time has flown, like birds from a nest.

Chalo, leave it! What's the use of talking about them any more?

Susan, get me the needle and thread from the sewing basket ...

No, let it be. Get me a hank of wool. I shall roll it into balls. My fingers will become stiff if I don't do something.

Taking a deep breath.

– Ladki, my hands are numb. My fingers are becoming moist.

The daughter bends and touches her hands.

– What is this, Ammu! You're running a fever.
– Pain, such terrible pain, child. Ladki, death is ruthless. It collects its dues, for all the days gone by, for all the days to come. It never leaves out anything.

My back is laid out on thorns. The lacerations are deep. I am sure there are new eruptions ...

Susan, turn me on my side and see what new nuisance has exploded there. What misery! I'm sure there's pus right down the back bone.

Susan and the daughter both bend over and scrutinize Ammi's back.

– What a large swelling! It's full of pus too. The doctor must see it. Ammu, why didn't you tell us earlier?
– Keep quiet, don't unlock this mouth of mine.

But tell me, looking after me, is it not Susan's duty? And yours? Susan has been changing the bed sheets. Has been making entries in the chart, correct, incorrect, whatever. I had fever yesterday also.

– Ammiji, it is my mistake. Please forgive me.

– I won't say anything. Doctor sahab will tweak your ears ...

A patient who's dependent on others is dead even before death arrives.

Seeing her daughter pick up the telephone.

– Let it be, child. Doctors have no more cures for me. They only pretend ... creating false hopes!

Slowly, as if to herself.

– This iron frame hurts. My back too. It's an old casing. Who knows where all it's given way. I want to know what all has happened to me.

The daughter, drawing near.

– Ammu, how these bedsores bother you!

– All my life, my body enjoyed the bed and now that very bed is doing me in. Time! Ladki, listen. When all resources are exhausted, this storehouse of energy too packs up. That's what they call old age.

Susan, make the bed later. First sponge my face and hands.

Susan, wiping Ammu's face with a towel.

– Ammiji, I hope you've pardoned me, na?

– Make up with your sister, or she'll surely get rid of you.

She's made of stone. My other daughters have taken after their father. They can neither be harsh towards anybody nor bear any harshness. But this daughter of mine has taken after her mother's family.

Both laugh.

– Susan, first do my hair. Then give me my spectacles from the cabinet so I can see your flustered face.

Actually if you think about it, how are you to be blamed for this new misery? Your carelessness is limited; you only failed to observe what was happening to the patient.

The daughter finishes her conversation with the doctor.

– Ammu, you were in so much pain, you should have told us, na?
– Ladki, let the patient retain some self-respect, at least. Need I have groaned in order to let you know?

There, Doctor sahab has arrived. That's how he rings the bell. I can tell from the pressure of his hand on the bell. He's a doctor, after all. The bell goes on ringing.

Listen ladki, all movements stop at this point. And then start again. That's nature! Always.

– Ammiji, how are you? What's the news?
– Son, I am not going to say that I'm well. That'd be insulting the doctor and his medicine.

The doctor takes the temperature and then examines the abscess on her back.

– It is spreading merrily, beté. Now you'll have to make a new diagnosis. It seems this body has learnt a new trick.
– When did the pain start?
– It has increased over the past two days. Before that, it was bearable. You're not going to cut me open again, are you?
– Ammiji, there's a lot of pus here. Let's drain it. You will get some relief.
– Beta, leave something with me to pay my toll tax with. I don't want to be stranded at the checkpost.
– Ammiji, don't move. And what is this about toll tax?
– All vehicles are stopped at the Shimla barrier. It seems that I'm standing there. Let's see when my car will pass through the checkpost.

Now only that remains.
– There will be some pain, Ammiji ...
– You go ahead. I'll bear it. As a child, I breezed through life on my own But this wind is mighty. It can uproot even well-rooted, ancient trees.

How much longer will it take, Doctor sahab?
– Not very long.
– Beté, what's the use of sending people like me to the moon while we are still alive? We'll just turn to manure out there when one day soon a human being may be born there.

– Ammiji, there's not enough oxygen there. All the countries of the world are busy exploring the moon. Perhaps they will find a solution.
– Doctor sahab, may I take some brandy mixed in milk? The pain has taken a toll on my energy.
– Susan, bring some milk for Ammiji with a little chocolate in it.
– Doctor sahab, for years I weighed only fifty kilos. Even when I had children, I didn't allow an inch of fat to accumulate. Regular pace of life. Everything as per routine. No fried or oily food. I took a tonic only when heavy with child, Vincharnis! I was never lazy. I'm only wanting to complete my quota of the rations ...
Doctor sahab, how long will you keep me here?
– Ammiji, take rest. Eat whatever your heart desires. And no worries, no anxieties.

Ammu, with a smile.

– So, you've opened the gates at last! ... My throat gets very dry, beta. May I take cold things?
– Why not? Milk, yoghurt, ice cream, whatever you like. But it will be better if you take only warm things today.

Handing over the prescription to Susan.

– Once before going to sleep and then once every four hours. Call me if she feels any discomfort. Achcha Ammiji, may I take your leave now?

– May you live long, beta. Earn well. Stretch out the lives of your patients.
– Ammu, why are you saying all this to the doctor?
– Don't misunderstand, ladki. For the patient, the doctor is like one's very own. One says what comes to mind. This lightens the heart as also the pain. Isn't it so, Doctor sahab?

The doctor smiles.

– All right, Ammiji. If you have a problem, don't wait, just call me.
– If my doctor daughter-in-law doesn't take it amiss ...

Laughter.

The daughter returns after seeing the doctor to the door.

– Ammi, the doctor appeared embarrassed at your remark about stretching out the life of his patients.
– No, ladki, he knew that I was only joking.
– Ammu, are you feeling better now? Hope there's nothing on your mind? No anxieties, regrets.
– No. Some things in life are salty and some others sweet. That's all. What's there to regret? Life's blueprint brings bright and dark phases for each one of us. Joy and sorrow, gain and loss, ups and downs, each plays itself out in turn. No one's life is an eternal celebration

with firecrackers. Everything slides into each other, the good, the bad, the unpleasant. Only the one above can stop this flow.

But remember. Only the one who makes a boat can ride it to sea. Those who work shall reap the fruit. That's life. The accomplishment of the living.

My journey has stretched a little too much.

– Ammu, if you like, we could arrange a paath?

– That's a good idea. Scriptures are like ambrosia, they calm the mind. But let's just have the recitation followed by the sankirtan songs. Don't let's get into the whole rigmarole of rituals. Do only what's required ...

What's that fragrance from the kitchen? Is someone making halwa? Ladki, amongst food lovers, halwa has the pride of place. It has innumerable attributes.

– The halwa you make on Sankranti is incomparable.

Ammi pursuing her own train of thoughts.

– Ladki, these days your nana's nature seems to fill me. When he, my father, was close to death, he would call out repeatedly –

Arré, what delicious aroma is this? It's suji being fried over a slow fire, na? Bring it, bring it, if it's ready. Come on, hurry. Don't delay.

All those present would smile, but your nani would get really anxious ...

Your grandmother, she with the name of dawn, took great care of your nana.

Ladki, this stage of life too is important. Silence begins to descend on man. If he looks within, he'll see a junkyard, heaped high with old stuff. Something comes to mind and starts off a search within.

Why are you getting up? Sit for some time more.

Ladki, some people get caught in the net of attachments. Look at me, I am still so involved in your life. Lying here, all I think of is you:

She's gone out, She's come back. What is She thinking? What is She doing?

The time that is to come will bring its own anguish with it.

– Ammu, don't linger over any thought that's unpleasant.

– You're right. It is neither easy nor possible to feel about in the air with your hands. Memories are the earnings of a lifetime. Now all the days I get are a bonus ...

Ladki, just see if there's a diya lying somewhere. Keep it handy. Where all will you look for it when it is needed?

I don't see your brother. I have been waiting for him since yesterday. What's the matter?

– Ammu, he has gone out of town. On tour.

– Ladki, why this sudden need for deception? There were toffees and peppermints under my pillow this morning. He alone thinks of such things. Even when I was not ill, he used to leave chocolates for me in the fridge.

Daughter, why do you send him on tour? Your brother's heart is pure and simple. He is taken in easily. He must've been held back. Wives sit at home with life's sieve, fishing for faults. Pull this one out. Hunt that one. Who knows what all they will find after I'm gone.

– Mamu, let it be.

– Chalo. This too is not important. But don't try to distract me with excuses. Up there, ladki, the Book of Life must be open at the last chapter.

Laughs.

– As a child, your brother was fat and chubby. He had curly hair. He was absolutely charming when he smiled his mischievous smile. He would return from his school and immediately sit down with his books. Question him and he'll say –

I need to learn this all up.

Do you understand what I am thinking? He's finalizing the sequence of questions and answers.

– No, Ammu. Don't think so. Bhai attends to so many things for you without show or fuss.

– Why shouldn't he? He's my son. Can't sons love their mothers? The bond is always there. They pretend as if they have long forgotten their mothers. It pleases their wives. Mothers are relegated to a long gone past.

The same string of queries repeated again and again,

Why didn't you tell me? After all, why didn't you remember it? Why didn't your mother say this? Why did she not do that? Why did she not give me this at the right time?

Ammu smiles.

– Recriminations and quips, annoyance and acrimony ... all these are parts of the game. It doesn't pay to be always sweet and nice.

Ladki, do you think your brother will reach here in time to perform the last rites.

– Ji, Ammi.

– Ladki, that is the way of the world. When the old rafters shake, it raises a huge wind. The usual calculations, practical considerations, opposing advice, opinions ... The path will emerge below your feet in whichever direction you walk.

Ladki, it appears that the moistness within me has dried. My heart is in agony like a fish out of water. Sand. Only sand wherever I cast my eyes.

– Ammu, should I ask for fruit juice or sheera?

Ammu smiles.

– I have only one chant. Halwa.

– With some crushed almonds added to it?

– You have stolen the words from my mouth. That is just what I was about to say.

Ladki, somewhere, somehow, the two of us are matched, our melodies in tune.

Ammu keeps looking at Susan for sometime, then starts dozing.

Opens her eyes. To herself.

– All waters pull to the rivers
All rivers to the ocean
So life towards liberation
Mukti!

Wonder how much time and distance I have left. After all, this is only a wayside halt.

Like the sound of rainfall in one's sleep, I hear the sounds of a time past.

Old woman, you have completed all your tasks. Bas, all that remains to cast away is the body.

The daughter enters the room with a bowl in her hand.

– Ammu, let it cool down a bit. It's very hot.
– Look ladki, something flickers on the windowpane behind you.

Daughter casts a quick look.

– Ammu, there is nothing there.

– You won't be able to see it. I can. A day from the past shimmers on the window.

It was raining heavily that day. Still a long time to dusk. I had finished my work and was standing at the window, looking at the hills. The thunder, the fleeing clouds, the lightning. Water gurgled and streamed down from the tin roof.

I saw someone, wearing a mackintosh, come up the hill.

I looked carefully. It was your pitaji. Standing there, it was him I had been thinking of. I quickly opened the door. He said –

I hadn't knocked yet. How did you open it for me?

I saw you coming. I felt as though you were walking, holding the finger of an unknown child.

Your pitaji was solemn at first, then he laughed –

Do you feel lonely during the day?

No. Not lonely. But you must have seen what was on my mind.

Change your clothes. I'll get you tea.

Ladki, why are you looking depressed? I haven't kept anything back from you. I found that day in the maze of memories.

The mind has its own ways. Ladki, water burns. Even snow melts. Sunlight is not a doe that gambols lightly. Sunlight is reined in by the sun so even the earth is enamoured of it.

Are you listening? When, for the first time, new earrings are put in the ears of a daughter, she looks very pretty. A tagadi around the little son's waist looks still prettier. And the first innocent smile on the lips of a child is very charming. To see with one's own eyes the first steps of tiny feet is the prize of life, ladki.

I can see your father clearly. He is feeding honey to the child on his lap. Sometimes drops of grape juice. Sometimes he touches the child's lips with a pomegranate seed with such absorption as if there is nothing in this world beyond this play of life.

Ladki, this is not maya or an illusion. No, no. Life and living are not imagined. It is the leaving of it that is. Is there anyone of flesh and blood who can savour juicy mangoes, ripened on the trees, after his death? Nahin ri. No one made of the five elements water, air, earth, sky and fire.

Ladki, this world is absolutely enchanting!

The daughter touches her mother's hand.

– Wind, shadows, rain, light, darkness, the moon and the stars ... the games this world plays are unique. Magical!

Next morning on waking.

– The doctor has given me great relief, Susan. I slept comfortably through the night. I can put up with minor aches and pains. But the suffering of these last two days has crushed me. I had become very irritable.

I don't know what all I've been saying to you.

The daughter, pouring tea into a cup.

– Ammu, you have tremendous control over yourself. I couldn't have borne so much suffering.
– Ladki, giving birth to a child alone makes one familiar with the finer shades of pain.
– Ammu, why such hurtful words?
– Pain too comes in many shapes and forms. Slight pains, sharp pains, piercing pain. Ladki, the game of life is contained in it.

Seeing the daughter smile.

– Once a woman's body passes through the storm of childbirth, her nerves and muscles get toughened.

But how could you have acquired this capacity to endure such pain.
– Leave me out, Ammu, tell me when you conceived your first baby ...

Ammu with enthusiasm.

– I was alert. I did my daily chores with the usual attention. Ladki, making a baby is like performing a yagna. During those days, a woman draws energy from the whole cosmos to recharge herself. She feels that special kind of existence that is hers. She watches the skies within her, even as she creates life, becoming one with nature, its textures and rhythms.

– Ammu, what happened when the baby was about to be born?

– I was making tiny frocks for the baby, when movement started inside. Your pitaji was getting ready to go to bed. I said –

You can't sleep tonight. You have to call Jacob quickly.

– Then?

– Then what? All the preparations had already been made. The moment the doctor entered, my first daughter arrived.

– Ammu, you must have been sad to see that it was a daughter.

– Don't try to be clever, ladki! Ask yourself. Were you and your sisters treated any differently from your brothers?

– No, Ammu, never. But it is not so for all girls. The birth of a daughter brings gloom.

– Ladki, your parents never made any such distinctions. Listen, it is important for a mother to give birth to a daughter cast in her own image. It is an act of great faith. A daughter makes the mother immortal; she never dies thereafter. She is here today. She will be here tomorrow. From one generation to another, from mother to daughter to daughter's daughter, and so on and on, that is the source of all life in our universe.

– Ammu, say something in praise of the father.
– The blood of fathers runs in the veins of his children. All praise to him, devotee of the goddess of the night! It is by his grace that the lamp of the family is lit. That's the law of nature. It invests the father with the power to provide the seed of life, but keeps him out of the process of shaping the body. The father stands outside even as the mother gives birth to their child. That's why the mother is called Janani, lifegiver. It is she who makes the baby's body grow with her mind and in her body.

The daughter, smiling.

– Ammu, you're speaking the language of books.
– So what if I haven't read the great Patanjali? Knowledge can be imbued by hearing, seeing as well as through experience.
– Ji Ammu!
– Every man considers himself to be supreme. Do you know why? Because he is blessed with the musk of life. Ladki, life is like a deer, a musk deer, a kasturi mrig. It spreads its perfume through this transient world and flits away instantly.

The woman holds this fleeting deer for a few moments and becomes the creator.

This is the play of creation. From here starts the cycle of generations ... an unbroken chain of progeny.

Ladki, the soul of the world resides in this. The body dies, not the soul. Water dries, but not blood. It flows in one's children, and in their children.

– Ammu, the male deer ...

– The male deer has a deep desire to have a son. This desire occupies his whole being. It is ingrained in his nature and in his inclinations. Being a father, he thinks of sons, grandsons, great grandsons: a whole line of male descendants. Ties up the family into a neat parcel.

Are you listening? What are you thinking about? A family doesn't come about by mere wishing. You earn it in your previous lives, the fruit of good deeds done. Ladki, a father is like a reservoir of water. He provides the sap generation after generation to the family tree. A son's claim on a father is less than that of the grandson. He may turn away from the family, but he never neglects his duty.

Ammu with a smile.

– I can see the way to mukti and freedom, ladki. I need something to wet my throat. If you're giving me something cold, let it be nimbu pani. Otherwise hot tea.

The daughter places the tea tray on the table.

– Well done. I wanted something cold, but the urge was for tea. Ladki, experience, reading and thinking do sharpen the intelligence. But life alone gives it meaning. Thoughts

spring from the mind and the mind rests in the soul.
– And the heart, Ammu?
– The heart is a monkey. The soul alone is pure and true, conscious and aware. Awareness is like water, pellucid and clear, presiding deity of this body.
– Mamu!

Suddenly, with asperity.

– Enough of sermons! Now let me rest.

The daughter gets up and moves towards the door.
Ammu calling out.

– Come back. Let me finish what I was saying.

The daughter sits down in her chair again.

– Ji, Ammu. Carry on.
– The same waters in which a man bathes brings fertility to the woman too. He shatters the night into fragments. She strings these fragments of night to make a garland for herself. For her, making a baby is like wearing a jewel. This is why a mother is blessed. The soul emerges out of the waters of her sequestered lake to enter the body of the new life inside her.
– Ammu, you've put it so beautifully!
– Ladki, that is how a mother defeats death. Do you understand? Only one who is not blessed with the fruit of a good life is perishable.

The daughter, stares sadly at the ceiling.

Ammu, annoyed.

– What are you looking at? How will you find anything if nothing is there. Go and read the book that has been allotted to you. That is what you'll have to do all your life.

That is all you will do.

Long silence.

– Ladki, a pitcher full of water is better than a vast desert. There is nothing in your account book, absolutely nothing.
– Ammu, let it be. Let's come back to the father.
– By becoming a father, man finally loses out. No longer does he receive his due pleasure from the woman with a child. She becomes mother. This is fundamental knowledge. But even without that, you surely know that the soul and body weave together the romance of this world. Alone they aren't worth much. I hope you understand this much?

The daughter, irritated.

– No, I don't understand a thing!
– Ladki, it is not just a matter of love and longing; there is a lot more to it. Tell me frankly. Has someone known you, or what you desire? Has someone desired you?

The daughter remains silent.

– If you can't compromise, don't know how to yield, who will come forward to hold you, child? Today you are where you were yesterday. Tomorrow also you will be where you are today. Am I not talking sense?
– Yes Ammu.
– Ladki, the company of someone dear makes a tremendous difference to one's life. There is joy within and without.

Say something. Or am I to be the only one to say everything. Unless your feet make the effort to climb up the steps, Ladki, how can any gain accrue? Miss an opportunity of coming together once, and you may have to wait for several lives.

When she sees her daughter smile, her tone becomes soft.

– I am saying all sorts of things. If fate is well disposed, opportunities arise by themselves.

The daughter breaks into laughter. Ammu, in a subdued voice.

– A sparrow has just flown past me. It'll fly into the fan. No, it's not a sparrow; it's a rabbit. Catch it and give it to me, otherwise it will run away, far far away.

Susan, bending over her.

– Ammi, may I change your wet clothes?
– So, it has finally occurred to you. You do as you please, you change the bed sheets whenever you please, hand

over my medicine, write up the chart. That's your job. Otherwise you don't pay attention to your work.
– No, Ammiji, that isn't true.
– Susan, are you cooking mutton? Just the thing I want to have today. My back feels cold. I like that fragrance of the frying. Ladki, good that you didn't order yakhni today. Otherwise I would've felt like leaving today itself.
– Ammu, why do you say such things again and again?
– You're right. I've caught the nomad's disease. I'm obsessed with the thought that I shall have to go, I have to go. Ladki, when the one above has noticed a person who's waiting at the departure gate, it doesn't take him long to announce the date of departure. But tell me. The shahtoot will ripen next month, won't they? How many days are there to next month?
– Just ten, Ammu.

Ammu with concentration, counts on her fingers.

– One, two, three, four, five, six ... There's still time, ladki. Many more days yet.

The daughter gently presses her mother's forehead.
Ammu, with alertness.

– You have seen birds flying in the sky, haven't you? And seen the green shoots bursting from the branches? You must have also felt the breeze of the changing seasons? Have you walked barefoot on grass wet with dew? And basked in the mellow sun of winter?

Ladki, this world is full of such infinite blessings. There are pleasures in this world other than the pleasures of the bed. You know that, don't you?
– Ji, Ammu.
– Never feel sorry for yourself. Keep despair at an arm's length. I am not anxious for you. You can neither be tormented nor can you torment anybody. But think and tell me, child, when the need arises, whom will you call?

The daughter, after a long silence.

– I won't have the need. But I will respond if someone calls me. Are you satisfied now?
– Ladki, you are the child of my heart. Beneath this stony hardness, there must be springs of water.

The daughter, petulantly.

– Ammu, there's no need to talk about such things. I am what I am and will remain so!
– All right, I agree with you. But bear my words in mind ... There is no need to allow an outsider to enter your life now. No one can be forced to run. Only he who runs on his own is called a runner.
– Not everyone can.
– A self-reliant person needs a vast sky and an immeasurable earth. Don't bother about trivial things.

Those who restrain their heart's desires, see a limited sky. Their race ends with their homes and hearths. They go on making piles of chapattis, keep spinning spider's webs.

Are you listening? There's not much on offer in this either.

– Ammu, let's talk about something else.

– I won't come back to tell you all this. You are not subservient to anyone. You are independent. Ladki, that is your strength, your capacity, your power. Do you understand?

– Ji.

– All my life I've been hearing members of your family say Ji, Ji. Soft words. I know exactly what they mean. I was eighteen when I got married. Your father was a handsome, well-built man, pure of heart. We got along splendidly. Imagine, where and when I started life.

Tell me something, ladki, why do you people consider yourselves a cut above others? In families, decay usually sets in by the third generation. It is not good that family pride should turn one's head.

– Ammu, every family has its own memories.

– Yes, I know. In the life histories of families, the sun doesn't rise and set at the same time. It cannot. See, I'm lying here in front of you, aren't I! Can you from somewhere bring back that fresh young girl in her bridal dress? Can you? No you can't. You can't.

After a short pause.

– Ladki, your mother looked beautiful as a bride. People adored her. How one changes with time! There is a time for going up the ladder. And a time for coming down. No one remains beautiful forever.
– Ammu, after marriage, how did you find this new family?
– Don't be too proud of that family of yours. When I arrived, the fortunes of your family were already in decline. There was no lack of pride and vanity though there was a lot of humility and gentleness also. The grandeur of the large mansion had faded somewhat. It poured in some places but the roof held.
– Ammu, tell me some more about my father.
– Once the decline sets into families, it continues till it has run its course. Your father was very calm by nature. Sober. I was a bit stern. But I was keen to learn and I did. I learnt a lot from him.

Ammu, suddenly agitated.

– Ladki, why are you making me chew the same old cud all the while? Are you trying to distract me or amuse yourself? Age deprives one of all grace. Its darkness engulfs all human beings. I'm a burden on all of you. Where was the need for such a long life!

My daughter's son died at the age of twenty seven. Oh!

How handsome, tall and well-formed he was! It was a terrible blow. But there was no appeal, no protest against that. Neither here, nor up there. He didn't die, he was murdered.

Ladki, just show me his photograph. I can see him standing right in front of me now. You were needed here very much, child! Why were you snatched away? It was the day of your engagement. Your fiancee, bedecked in her finery, kept waiting. The ring never reached her finger.

Ladki, there's someone else who makes us play this game. And see what my other grandson, his elder brother, did. He followed the same road as if to challenge fate. He brought the same girl home, as the promised daughter-in-law of the family. They spared no effort to take care of you, beti Chitra. But your share of life was over! It was all over within a year. You couldn't even fondle to your heart's content the one you gave birth to.

Susan, put something in my eyes. I don't know why they are watering. They've become very old, these eyes of mine.

– Ammiji, will you have chocolate-Horlicks or tea?

– Whatever you like. Has Didi gone away from here?

– She has gone to lie down for a while, Ammiji.

– Cover me with the sheet, Susan.

– Sheet? But it is very hot, Ammiji!

– Do what I tell you to. You don't know anything about

the music or the rhythm of this song. You stick to your own timetable.

Gave the medicine.

Changed the dressing.

Gave the injection.

Took the temperature.

Rang up the doctor.

Turned the patient over.

Why are you smiling? Your records will go into the wastepaper basket. Everybody's record goes there.

– Ammiji, I'll get the Horlicks.

– No, no! You should attend to my head first. It feels hollow inside. Put some oil in my hair, Susan.

Susan massages oil into Ammi's hair.

Ammi closes her eyes.

After a nap.

– Hasn't she got up? Is Didi still sleeping?

– Ji.

– My nails are bothering me. Cut them.

– Ammiji, I cut them only yesterday.

– You may have, but do as I say. Just to please me.

Are your brothers married, Susan?
– Yes, both of them.
– Do you send money to your parents?
– Yes.
– Have you selected anyone for yourself? You have to find one yourself.
– No, Ammiji, not yet. I want to do a course in nursing first.
– Good idea, Susan. Stick to it. Don't drop it midway. Surely you have a friend or two?

Susan smiles.

– You don't spend too much on him, I hope?

Susan, laughing.

– No, Ammiji.
– Listen to me. See that neither you nor he bear the entire expenses. You should share them. Otherwise you'll find yourself being taken for a ride. You understand that, don't you?
– Ji, Ammiji.
– Susan, after marriage, don't become a plaything in anyone's hands. Be strong ...

Somebody just rung the doorbell. See who has come. Who is it?
– Nobody, Ammiji.
– Go and see again. It's time for Shobha Ram to come.
– Ammiji, he has been in the kitchen for quite some time.

– Find out if the kheer is ready. We talked about it in the morning, remember?

– Ammiji, pranaam!
– May you live long. Jité raho, beté.
– The kheer is ready. Will you taste it?
– Bring me some. Just two spoonfuls.
– Here. I have added some roasted nuts.
– You know, don't you, that I still have my original teeth and they're strong.
– Ammiji, should I make puas this evening?
– No, no. Kheer itself is pretty heavy. Someday I'll tell you what goes well with what. The fines and challans I have got for not knowing that.

The daughter, standing close to her.

– What's this about challans, Ammu? I'm curious. Do tell.
– Shobha Ram, the kheer is delicious. Keep preparing halwa, puri, pakodas, kheer, puas and keep feeding everyone. But remember you have one more task to perform. Don't make any excuses. You have to escort Ma up to that place.

The daughter, light-heartedly.

– Ammu, what was that about the challans?
– Nothing special. Squabbles over food and cooking, what

else. Whenever there was a long argument on that subject, I had a solution. I would place the tea tray before your pitaji –

Here, the tea is waiting for you. Please have it first.

Your father appreciated good tea. It would make him forget everything else.

– Ammu, did you really have so many clashes with him?

– Perhaps. I don't remember much. Why do you provoke me? Is it necessary to know everything?

– What's the harm if I do, Ammu?

– Ladki, everyone's life passes through a series of points and counterpoints. But in a family, the game is never amongst equals. The master of the house provides for the family, and he grows in strength and authority. The mother of his children is mortgaged to this authority.

– Ammu!

– Yes, after marriage, a woman becomes the boatman of the family. You have seen boats and shikaras floating in the lake, haven't you? The family enjoys the ride, while the woman works at the oars. She rows the shikara throughout her life. Her situation improves only when she starts earning her own livelihood.

Now this is worth thinking about. A man works, and gets his just returns. A woman toils day and night and earns nothing. She loses herself in bonds and attachment. Unknowingly. Unaware. If she doesn't look after herself, who is going to look out for her?

– Ammu, this is sheer activism!
– Quiet, ladki. You are so quick to pounce upon my words. Why? I know your tricks very well. The journey's mine, the learnings yours.

Looking towards the window.

– Change these heavy curtains. Let some fresh air come in. Ladki, let me be quiet for some time. My own past is unfolding within me.

Ammu closes her eyes.

After some time.

– Still here? Tell me, ladki, what are you doing in this world? Show me a single bit that you've earned in this life. What is your capital? On top of that you want to judge what I have done?

The daughter, getting up.

– I'm going.
– No. No, please sit down. Keep me company. I'll talk of things that interest you. I have very little time left.

Tell me, where do you stand? At which crossroads? Do you have anyone awaiting you? You stand outside the doors of your siblings.

– Ammu, not the same thing again ...
– Don't interrupt me, ladki. Let me see things clearly. See, I have a son and daughters, grandsons and granddaughters, a whole family and yet I'm alone. And you? You're outside that timeworn tale in which there is a husband, children and a family.

You don't have the hassles of a family life, you are you, full in yourself. Ladki, to be yourself is the ultimate, the best. If you too had to run a family, you would've realized by now that all the glory of a family life lies in the superficials – as someone's wife, daughter-in-law, mother, nani or dadi. And again the same everydayness of food, clothes, jewellery. Ladki, a woman is queen only in name. Sheltered and ensconced, she is wiped of all individuality.

The daughter, smiling.

– Ammu, your arguments are unimpeachable!
– If you think carefully, there's an answer to every question.
– Susan! Get some juice for Ammu and for me too.
– Right action girl. Pouring your sap on something which is dry.
– Susan, make mine really cold. My throat is parched.

– That was nice, Susan. My thirst is quenched. Go have some too.

Ladki, you have no idea how much tact a woman within a family has to have, how much restraint. You are free. No one restrains or controls you. You do as you please. But remember, one needs to be independent of one's own self too. Do you ever let yourself go? I'm not talking about impulses. Have you ever been able to do something that you really wanted to do?
– Ammu, what should I say?

Long silence in the room.

– I ran this house with clockwork precision, but I did nothing purposeful or important for me, my self.
Daughter, how much I regret this now.

The daughter, surprised.

– What was it that you wanted to do, Ammu?
– I wanted to climb tall mountains, reach limitless peaks. But this did not fit into the scheme of things domestic. Who could I have said this to? Your father? He could barely cope with the family pinpricks. Besides, he loved his punctuality; everything on its time, not a minute early, not a second late. I turned myself into a clock for him.

The daughter looks out of the window.
Susan starts folding the clothes.

Ammu snapping.

– What are you folding those clothes for? Piling up the washing. It's not as if a new baby has arrived in the family. Only this old woman is leaving. Pile up her old clothes ...

The daughter gets up and puts on a record.
Ammu listens to the sitar music for a while with wonder. Then in vexation.

– Stop it! This noise is too much for me. Understand, will you? My veins have dried up.

Music plays havoc with my body ...

What are these black threads unravelling in front of my eyes? Ask someone!

As Susan tries to cover her, Ammu, with a start.

– Why are you people troubling me? Pull the curtains apart. Let in some fresh air. Hurry up. I'm feeling suffocated.

Why are you silent?

Listen to me. Listen.

I'm not asking for a butterfly. I'm only demanding my rights. Give them to me. Let me breathe fresh air.

Susan draws the window curtains apart.

– Ammiji, the glare will bother you.
– A cave! This is a cave! Why have you imprisoned me? Open the doors. Who has bolted them? Call the one

who is playing these tricks on me. Call my daughter. Take me to the balcony. I won't stay in this room even for a moment.

– Susan, give Ammi some Electral. I'll make a place for her in the balcony.

– Don't try to distract me, ladki. You have to make me sit in a chair. I don't want to lie down ... I won't lie down. I'll sit. Ladki, you must let me win today.

– Ammu, any movement will open the sores.

– Neither I nor my sores need your sympathy. Do as I say.

Susan places an easy chair in the balcony and spreads a mattress and a sheet on it. Places a cushion for support. Then both of them lift Ammi and take her out.

Ammu, after being seated in the chair, excitedly.

– What season is it now? The trees are still. Not a leaf moves. Which month is it?

The daughter, ignoring her, stands quietly, with her hands resting on the railing.

– I ask you. Answer me. Don't you dare ignore me.

– Ammi, it's the third week of May. There'll be dust storms soon. Look up, see the earth coloured sky. It looks so alien. Its strength has not been drained away by its grownup children. It looks like a thing past.

– Ladki, it seems the sky too has aged.

Ammu raises her head and looks at the electric poles. Then keeping her eye fixed on the trees below.

– These neem trees have a longer lifespan than the golden flesh-and-bone tree of man's life.
– Ammu, the neem trees are full of fresh leaves. The one outside your room has grown so tall.
– In this season, neem trees are full of fragrance. When they blossom, they give out a sweet smell. Their fragrance makes the daughters of the earth throb with desire.
– What then, Ammu?
– Arri, then what? They go to the ones who can satisfy their needs. These hazards and celebrations are connected to the body, aren't they? ... Ladki, I feel like a fish out of water again. The dampness at the edges is drying up. Terrible thirst. Give me some soda with ice cream.

And fetch one more chair. My son is about to come. He comes here straight from the office.

The daughter remains silent.

Ammu, to herself.

– A true woman must be able to subdue her man's mother ...
– Ammu, you too have passed through such a phase.
– I too must have done the same. All women do.
– Is it necessary?
– I suppose so. A woman puts her stamp on the mind and

body of her husband, possesses him. She has to. Otherwise she can have no peace and comfort.

Ammu smiles.

– Everyone's temperament is different. Some are more suspicious, some more trusting! Men understand this. That is the rule of family life, Give some take some. The one who gives must also take.

Susan feeds Ammu ice cream with a spoon.

– May you live long. I am satisfied.

Ammu, back in the room.

– This ice cream reminds me of the pistachio kulfi we had at Chandpal Ghat.
– What was special about it, Ammu?
– The time and the place. That place took one's breath away. Ships anchored in the waters. Sirens blaring. Lights glimmering on the water. The waves pushing each other up. Boats bobbing on the waters. The shores full of festivities. The sky stretched like a canopy over the heads of the living. Stars twinkling. The moon in full splendour. Ladki, the exuberance of life on earth and water was awesome.

Who would want to leave this earth after such a vision? But one has to depart when it is time.

When I had gone to Calcutta, I visited a number of places, Ladki. One evening my elder daughter took me and her little granddaughter there. Three branches of the family had come together. You can call them three generations. The daughter of my grandson, my daughter and I.

Ladki, children in families rejuvenate the old. We elders are always conscious of age at first, but soon lose ourselves in the children.

That evening, your sister acted as though she was the elder one and I, her mother, the younger.

But that naughty granddaughter of hers, an only child, said that her papa's nani was not only old but also a child.

She begged me again and again –

Nani-amma, have one more ice cream, please come, let us share it half-half ...

When time and place are right, the pollens of families mix and melt into each other.

Wait ladki, I can see something through the lacings of my heart ...

– What is it, Ammu?

Ammu gives a toothless smile.

– A horse. Fleet-footed. Strong. You haven't done any horse riding, have you? You've neither reined in a horse, nor let go of yourself. Ladki, god favours she who understands her times. Only the hand that earns, knows what and where to give.

The daughter looks beyond the walls and closes her eyes.

– If you are feeling bored, why don't you go for a walk?

The daughter leaves and comes back after changing her clothes.

– Ammu, I'm going out for a cup of coffee. Do you want me to bring back something? Pineapple pastries?
– Yes please. Come back when you like. Don't worry about me. I'll be here ... Yes. If you are going to the hairdressers, ask her to come and trim my hair too. It weighs me down. I'll feel free.
– Susan, keep everything, the towels, shampoo, hair oil, ready. She won't have much time. If she comes before I return, get Mamu's hair trimmed.
Ammu, is that all right?
– Yes.

Have you noticed, Susan? That is my girl. She leaves and the room has lost its cheer.
– Ammiji, Didi loves you very much.
– She not only loves me but also understands me. There is a difference between the two. It is one thing to love,

quite another to understand. She is always sensitive to the needs of others.

Susan, your Didi looks rather distracted. I don't know what is bothering her.
– Nothing, Ammiji, she gets tired.
– Will you be able to take care of her after I'm gone? She needs a lot of rest. When she works, she forgets everything else. She is not afraid of hard work. It'll be good if you stay on. Susan, she seems to be hard and dry on the outside but she gives everyone his or her due.

Do me a favour, Susan. Go outside and see the colour of the sky. Are there any signs of rain? Once it rains, I'll bathe in the open and be washed clean. My back is in a bad shape. Medicines, bandages and who knows what else ...
– The sores appear to be healing, Ammiji.
– Don't you fool me. You see the sores when you dress them. I can't. Still, I know better than you because I bear the pain.

Smiling.

– Let it be. Now tell me, have you ever had a bath in a river. Cold and hot showers are nothing in comparison. I have bathed in a baoli, a river, a lake and in the sea. What joy! Such happiness! I bathed in the sea at Puri once to my heart's content. My elder daughter took me there.
– Ammiji, you keep thinking of Badi Didi?

– Why shouldn't I? She is my first born. There were lots of boys in my in-laws' family. There was great rejoicing when she arrived.
– And your youngest, Ammiji?
– She is very intelligent. But once she gets annoyed, it is very difficult to bring her round. Parents pass on their qualities and eccentricities to their children. The soil they grow in and the culture they imbibe influence their being.

Listening carefully.

– I hear something. See if there's somebody at the door. Must be my son.
– Ammiji, there's nobody at the door.
– Go and see again ... Maybe it's Prabha ... My eldest granddaughter takes after her father. How well she manages her affairs. Listen, Susan, you have met Mira, her younger sister, haven't you? She is so very elegant and so very charming. How often she comes to see me ...

Chalo, wipe my face with a cold towel. My neck too.

Susan, this neck of mine is not able to carry the weight of my hair any longer.

The daughter, returning home.

– Ammu, That's a good haircut. You're looking better.

– You have an outing, and I look more cheerful to you.

– No. Short hair suits you.

– Why didn't I think of this before. What relief! I am feeling lighter now ...

In those days, on their wedding day, the girl's hair would be braided such that it seemed as if all the world's constraints were woven into it.

When I arrived at my in-laws' house, your pitaji asked me at the very first opportunity –

Doesn't your plait bother you? Your head must be feeling very tight.

I said –

A single plait suits me better, but this is the custom.

Your pitaji said –

Look, there is no convention or custom in this family that can't be changed. Do whatever is comfortable and convenient.

– Ammu, how did you feel when you heard that?

– Good. It felt good. I thought I would be able to get along. Your father was gentle and disciplined. There were no unnecessary restrictions on me. But whatever was family tradition I had no freedom to modify or tamper. This was adhered to strictly.

– Ammu, but that is plain stubbornness!

– No, that's discipline. Your grandfather's sense of discipline and stability was amazing. Both father and son were almost alike in that. On either side, the scales were neither heavy nor light. I learnt about equality after coming to this family. In this family they didn't discriminate between boys and girls.

Listen to my words carefully, ladki. You are not the daughter of a family that discriminates.

– And Ammu, in your mother's family, my nana's?

– Let that be. There's no point in comparing the two.

– Tell me, please.

– Ladki, there was love and affection in your nana's family, plenty to eat and drink, plenty of time to play and dresses to wear. But even so, somewhere there was always a sharp line drawn between boys and girls. During your nana's last illness, we sisters used to take turns to be with him, but whenever he had to call someone, it would always be his son. It made me very sad. Why was there such attachment to a son? Ladki, at a time like this, one tends to lose track of things. Everything looks faded ...

What have I been saying? Let me think back.

Hahn ... Our brother was sent to college and we sisters were given lessons from a granthi and a maulvi. Just imagine, what I would have become if I had studied like my brother. And my children. The fact is that girls are prepared for a life of service. Your brother is studying. Go and give him milk. Bhai is sleeping. Go and cover him with the blanket. Hurry up. Place the plate of food before your brother. He is hungry. Bhai has eaten. Now you may.

Ammu is quiet for some time.

Susan bends close to her.

– What's the matter, Ammiji?

Ammu, in a nervous voice.

– My eyes are smarting. Smoke is spreading across them. What, what is happening?

The daughter rushes to the kitchen and returns quickly.

– It seems someone has smeared fog over my eyes. I am not able to see clearly.
– Ammu, this will give relief.
– What are you placing on my eyes?
– Mamu, these are pads of cream.
– Come close to me. The comfort you give to my eyes, have you ever experienced it yourself? Be honest with your mother, child.
– No, Ammu.

Silence hangs in the room for a long while.

Ammu, all of a sudden, unmindful of herself.

– When will the moon be full? When did the new moon appear? Tell me. I want to know.

The daughter, curtly.

– I know nothing about the phases of the moon.
– Is that why you carry this load on your shoulders? Throw it away. Hurl it far away. Don't turn your time to dust, ladki. Pull yourself up. Water flows downwards.

The daughter leaves the room.
Susan gives Ammi some glucose in water.
Ammi, to herself.

– When I conceived this daughter of mine, I don't know why I felt so lonely, so alone in my heart and mind. I felt like wandering alone on mountain paths. I felt as though a tall pine tree was growing inside me.

And it was indeed a tree that I gave birth to. It sways in the wind, just sways and dances. There is nothing in its future. But don't consider this girl to be cold. There's fire in her veins. She keeps herself under such control, I wonder how ...

Susan, the bell rang. Someone has come. Must be Biba and Bouba, my son's children.
– Ammiji, they have gone to their grandmother's.
– Hahn, to cheer up their nani. My samdhan must be

feeling disconsolate at the thought of my impending departure. The children must have gone to comfort her. Susan, you have met my grandson, haven't you? He is exactly like his dada sahab. He sits and gets up like him, moves his hands like him, even in his food habits ...

Ammi dozes off.

She opens her eyes and looks all around the room, as if trying to recognize it. Seeing her daughter standing near the bed, in a shrill voice.

– Who are you? You come in all tense and you charge out like a bullet. I've seen your face, I have. Taken after your father, have you? But ri, he wasn't at all arrogant. And you, you have a bag full of ego on your mind. That's why you never shared anything with anyone.

The daughter tiptoes out of the room.

– Susan, there is a piggy bank lying on top of the almirah. It is my granddaughter's. Don't misplace it. I've hung a bunch of silam yarn on the peg. I'm making a doll for her. I'll make the doll's hair with it. See that you don't tangle it.

Why are the shutters of the windows banging? Whose

odhni keeps fluttering in the wind? Oh! It is mine. Catch it. Otherwise it will be blown away by the storm.

Susan goes out and returns with Didi. Both of them bend over Ammi.

– She is asleep. She is in deep sleep.
– Susan, you rest for a while. I'll sit here.

Ammi, on waking up, in a sharp voice.

– Susan, where are you? Change my bedsheets. They are wet.

Susan cleans up Ammi and changes the bedsheets.

After a long deep sleep, Ammu wakes with a start.

– You hear the train, don't you? The station is quite some distance away, but the screeching sound of the engine reaches this far. It pierces deep into me.

The daughter runs a hand over her own hair.

– When your pitaji was preparing for his departure, he used

to sit up, startled by the four o'clock train. I would watch him silently. I never questioned him. What was there to ask?

One night, he sat up awakened by the vibrations, and resting his elbow against the pillow, bent towards me –

Can you hear that sound? It saddens me deeply!

I kept quiet. What could I say?

When the journey's nearing its end, god knows what different things knock at the heart. The many pleasures make one look back, while the soul pushes towards the infinite. And back again.

The daughter feels her mother's pulse on the pretext of adjusting the covering sheet.

Ammu, gently.

– This old timer is faring well. Go and take some rest.

The daughter, in order to avoid embarrassment.

– Ammu, I'm going to make coffee for myself. Shall I get a cup for you too?

– No. But if you wish, you may bring me some fresh fruit.

– Mango or Plum?

– Mango. Yes definitely aam! Hear the name, know its virtues. Ladki, your elder sister cuts fruit with great flair. She'll cut a mango in two, prick the halves with a fork and pour cream over them. Pleasing the eyes and the heart – steeping both in rich flavours.

– Ammu, you must have taught her.
– No. This delicacy is a characteristic of your family, not of mine.

The daughter, smiling.

– Ammu, what's all this talk about my family and your family?
– Why? What's so surprising about it? When a woman sets roots in her new home, she pushes the days at her parents' to the backyard of her mind. Look at your own mother. After a whole lifetime, I'm thinking of them now.
– Ammu, there's no fear of a clash now. Then how did this thought of comparison arise in your mind?
– Don't be naive. Where was the time to think or speak about these things? Now, lying here, I can see clearly the colours of the two, distinct each from each.
– So which side looks better, Ammu?
– Don't you boast, girl! My family was no less gifted.
– You come from the same branch. You kept all of us under firm control.
– No ri. Your family doesn't mix with anyone. It swallows up the good qualities of everyone.
– Don't say that. This family has been dancing to your tune for a long time.
– Whatever you have in your family, the pleasant and the unpleasant, is confused, scattered. I don't know what

your family sees and thinks. It always looked inwards.
– Ammu, do you find all of us like that?
– What else? Look at you. You were always like this. Ladki, my family was no less, but they never gave themselves such airs. In your family, everyone thinks no end of themselves. Here, everyone bears a little inscription.
– Ammu, why are you saying all this now?
– Let me. I won't be coming back again to tell you all this. The churning and crushing that a woman endures when she steps into a new family are no less than the upheavals of an earthquake. A woman stands up to them because she has no choice.
– Ammu, if you were to come into this family again, would you like it?

Ammu first scowls at her daughter and then beings to laugh.

– Arri, you old woman of this family ... If someone does ask me before sending me back to this world, I'll come back only to this family. Your ancestors have accumulated a rich tradition in this house. The family I have created is safely ensconced here, this is my own family. Why should I knock at somebody else's door?

The daughter restrains herself with some effort and kisses her mother's forehead.

– Years! I've lived in this world for years. But during these last few days, it has occurred to me repeatedly that

if I had known I was going to live for so long, I would have done something worthwhile with my life. This world is so huge, at least I could have gone around it. But I spent my days enmeshed in family responsibilities.
– Ammu, you've done so much. You've created a whole family.
– Don't exaggerate, ladki. I'm the mother of all of you, no doubt, but I, I am me. I'm not you and you're not me.
– But listen to me ...

Ammi, irritated.

– Your show of concern will not do me any good now. Children swallow up all the time allotted to their mothers.
– Ammu, surely you must get some satisfaction, some happiness from someone at least?
– I'm not talking of that. The mother produces. Nurtures with love and care. Then why is she alone sacrificed? The family divides her into fragments and scatters her to the four winds. Why? So that she may not remain whole, may not stand up in her own authority. A mother is kept either like a cow or a nursemaid. She should keep working, catering to the comforts of its members; that is all she is good for. She can conjure any image she wants of herself, but for her children she is no more than a housekeeper.

Susan switches on the table lamp behind Ammi's head and Ammi shuts her eyes.

Midnight.

Ammi, on waking.

– Susan, what time is it? Is it night, or is the day about to dawn?

– It is two o'clock at night, Ammiji.

– This night doesn't seem to move at all! Do something for my throat. I don't know what is happening. I have nothing to do. I just lie here and my memory leaps back across time. As if it is a speeding train.

Susan gives Ammu some water to drink.

– See if there is some misri lying around.

– I'll get it, Ammiji.

– The human body has been formed and structured to last a hundred years. I was doing all right. Had I not fractured my bone, I would have been fit.

– What is this, Ammiji? You've undone the dressing again?

– Yes, I've opened it. I've only untied what was tied.

Susan helps Ammi turn on one side, wipes the sores and starts applying the dressing again.

– Susan, listen to me. Let it remain open.

– Ammiji, the scabs will peel off. The sore will start oozing.

– Don't talk rubbish! Don't I know how much it hurts? I'm not wearing an armour; I'm sprawled on a bed of arrows.

– Susan, has the gaadi passed by?
– What vehicle, Ammiji?
– Susan, you're not doing your duty properly. You've become careless. You've been in this house for months, and you don't even know when the gaadi comes and goes.
– Ammiji, the station is far from here.
– I'm not speaking about the station. The gaadi which comes from the depot to pick up the empty milk bottles and then returns to deliver bottles of fresh milk.

Susan picks up the thermos.

– Ammiji, milk or Complan?
– Neither. I don't want anything. Just take me to Didi's room.
– I'll go and ask Didi.
– Ask Didi? Why? That room is also part of my house. Don't make me feel like a handicapped person. First take me to the small room so that I can offer my prayers, Then to Didi.

Susan picks up Ammi in her arms.

The daughter raises her head on hearing the sound of footsteps.

– Susan, what is this? What are you up to? Ammu? You here, at this time?
– Yes, haven't you gone to sleep yet? Ladki, do you mind if I lie down in your room and talk to you?

– No, Ammu.

The daughter places a cushion on the divan.

– Susan, carefully, here ... is it all right. Ammu?
– Yes! Have you started anything new?
– No Ammu. An old piece was lying unfinished, I thought I would look at it.
– Now stop thinking about too many things. Complete whatever you have in hand. Ladki, life is transient. But remember, do not consider this work any less important. This is also creation. Not inferior to the others. Life forces have a thousand channels. They may spring from anywhere and flow in any direction.

After a moment.

– You know, just as day and night get separated from each other, it seemed to me, as I lay there, that we mother and daughter too have drifted apart. I kept looking around to make sure that I was in the same room. I am still in my room. In this very world. Then I thought, why don't I go and see my daughter? So I came. Susan was not inclined to ...

Ammu smiles.

– The greatest blessing is to be able to do what one wants. Don't miss your ma too much. Only as much as is necessary. Go out for a few days. You're exhausted.

A long silence.

– Will you retain Susan?
– No, Ammu.
– And the cook?
– He'll also have to go.
– Can't you keep at least one of them?
– It'll be difficult.
– If you have vegetables, milk, curd and cottage cheese in the refrigerator, you can manage on your own somehow. Doing your own cooking and serving is refreshing in a way.
– Ji.
– You too must be thinking of the future? It's already too late, ladki. How will you manage alone?
– Somehow, Ammu.

Ammu, perplexed.

– If you are really determined, there's nothing that you can't do. There's nothing so small or so big that you can't manage.

The daughter keeps looking at her mother.

– Don't try to go against your grain.
– Ammu, if you have something important in mind, please tell me.
– No one is going to get jewellery, gold, cows, horses and fields from me. Only raw advice. Ladki, the headship of a family does not pass to a daughter. According to the sacred texts, your brother alone will wear the turban. And the

family flag will pass into the hands of the daughter-in-law ...

The key to the locker is in my cupboard. You'll find it in a round box on the upper shelf. Ladki, I had gold in kilos, now you'll find it only in grams. Whenever the need arose, it was used. You know ... I have prepared a will in my own hand. Show it to your brothers and sisters. Bahu has a locker of her own. Whatever belongs to her, is already with her. At the time of my departure, if her mother-in-law's gift does not reach her, I shall seek Bhavani's forgivenesss.

Families don't really possess all that they appear to have. What belongs to whom, why and how much, it's the same old story! The same topic of gossip among relatives. Don't argue with anyone. All the others are complete units in themselves, only you are outside every circle. Ladki, you are bound to find yourself alone.

The daughter lights a cigarette. With a smile.

– Ammu, want one?

– You'll have to raise my head with the help of the pillow.

– That's not a problem.

Ammu, relishing a smoke.

– If your heart tells you to do something, you must go ahead and do it. It was good that I came over here. If I hadn't, I would've continued to wander in the same darkness.

The daughter, light-heartedly.

– Ammu, it was really difficult to lift you off the bed. Susan wasn't wrong.
– Ladki, I just wanted to move from one room to another. I can't come back from the other world to see you even if I want to. Can I?
– No, Ammu.
– Several moments are entangled in this smoke. Ladki, may I ask you something?
– Yes, Ammi.
– Who owns this flat?
– Ammu, in my absence, it is yours.
– In that case ladki, I give it to you.

Both laugh together. Ammu in a strange, changed voice.

– If you ask me, it's not a matter for laughter but for tears.
– Ammu, it's not such a big issue that one should turn laughter into crying.
– It's not so small either that one shouldn't think about it at all. I see myself in you. The picture is more or less the same, although your temperament is more like that of your father's family.
– Is that a virtue or a flaw?
– Ladki, it's neither only a virtue nor only a flaw.

– You've put a seal of ambiguity on it. That doesn't prove anything.
– Ladki, what will you prove by travelling alone? When you live with someone, some things remain, some things get washed away. If you live alone, nothing remains, nothing is washed away.

Are you listening?
– Ji, Mamu.
– Ladki, in the midst of families lie the big and small pictures, the action spaces. There a woman sees herself even as she perceives others. When she becomes a mother, she lives through the past, present and future. Since you are not attached to a family, you live only for yourself, in yourself.
– What about the others, Ammu?
– Busy feathering their own nests. Ladki, the things you have done for this family won't bring you any compensation. Only your mother's blessings are with you.

Susan, peeping through the door.

– Shall we take Ammiji to the other room now?
– Susan, let Ammu stay here for some time. But yes, get some cold water, ice, a lemon and two glasses. You go and rest for a while. I'll wake you up if I need you.

Susan places a tray on the table.

– Ladki, your room looks full and thriving.

– That's because you are here, Ammu.

The daughter squeezes the lemon into the two glasses, adds ice and fills them up with water. Ammi looks on fixedly. The daughter places a cushion on the pillow and provides support to her mother.

– Ammu, will you be able to hold the glass?

– Yes, I'll hold it.

– Cheers, Ammu!

Ammu shakes her head. Taking a sip.

– Ladki, somewhere, sometime, we are sure to meet again. We'll recognize each other. Even in such a wide world, you can be sure of that. No matter where the mother is and where the daughter is, mother and daughter will always remain mother and daughter. Till the end of time.

The daughter restrains her tears and continues to look at her mother. Then she fixes her gaze on the glass, empties it in one gulp, refills it.

Next day.

Ammu is lying quietly. In no mood to talk. She removes the bangles from her wrists and pushes them under the pillow. Bundles up the sheet covering her and throws it on the floor. Removes the pillow from under her head and keeps it aside. Tosses the cushion towards the door. In an attempt to pull out the bedsheet from under her, she tosses her head right and left.

Susan, on entering the room.

– Ammiji, what are you doing?
– You can see what I am doing.
– Ammiji, you shouldn't ...
– One has to when it becomes necessary.
– I'll change the bedsheets, Ammiji.

Ammu starts taking her bandages off, quietly. Throws the cotton, gauze and bandages into the pan.
Susan goes and calls Didi.
The daughter, drawing near, in a gentle tone.

– Ammu, what are you doing?
– Exactly what you see.
– Pulling the bandages off like this will make the sores ooze again. Are you feeling hot?
– No, I'm feeling cold.

The daughter switches off the cooler. Ammu angrily.

– Hot or cold, whatever it is, now remove everything from here and put it outside.

Ammu tries to remove the chain from her neck.

– Remove it. I don't want it. I don't need anything now.

The daughter, lovingly.

– Ammu, not like this.

Ammu keeps staring with eyes opened wide.

– Ammu, anything you wish to have ...

Ammu, sharply.

– Quiet!
– Ammu, what is bothering you? Please tell me. Do tell me.

Ammu keeps looking towards the door for a long time. Then she signals to her daughter to come near her and says, as though whispering in her ears.

– Remove my body in the same way as I have removed the sheet covering me. Separate my body from me. I can't bear it anymore.

The daughter continues to bend over her mother. Alert. Silent.

– Do not keep my clothes in the house. Throw all of them out. Somewhere far away. So that you don't see them.

The daughter, in a flash, as though she has instinctively caught something from the inner recesses of her mother's mind, in a controlled voice.

– Ammu, things will be done according to your wishes. But you must listen to something I have to say. I will *not* give your clothes to anyone. *I* will wear them. Ammu, did you hear me? In this matter, even if you order me, I *will not* listen to you.

The tension on Ammu's face dissolves into the pillow.

The next morning Ammu appears alert.

– Susan, you are dragging your feet today. Didn't you sleep well last night?
– I slept well, Ammiji.
– Was I feigning sleep then? Susan, you sleep only if your patient sleeps. If the patient remains awake, you also have to keep awake.

Susan smiles.

– Listen to me, Susan. Come close. The papers have been signed. Now it's time to get ready. The documents too are ready. Susan, just go and peep outside. Can you see any patch of cloud in the sky?

Susan returns from the balcony.

– Ammiji, the sky is absolutely clear. No clouds. There is bright sunshine.
– Well, prepare my bath. Today I will not have my body sponged. I'll have my bath in the bathroom under the shower.
– Ammiji, shall I ask the doctor on the phone?
– No. His advice is limited to medication. His task is over. He is not the doctor of my body any more. Susan, there is the bigger doctor, high above these doctors. When the time comes, he collects the whole human being as his fee.

– Ammiji, let me wake up Didi.
– Let her sleep. A big task awaits her. It'll be good if she can have some rest.

Hahn, show me the soap you are going to use.

– Here it is, Ammiji.
– No. Not this. There's a box in my cabinet, take out a bar from it. That soap is specially meant for children. It doesn't dry the skin.

The daughter stands close by and looks on anxiously.

– Ammu, why not have some breakfast before you take your bath?
– As you please. What are you going to give me for breakfast today?
– Whatever you like. Mango juice, toast, egg, paratha, yoghurt, butter...

Ammu smiles.

– Are you trying to fatten me before sending me up? There's no hard labour waiting for me there. Ladki, this is the only place where one can use one's hands to create beauty and order. Up there, people don't have separate hearths in every household. Nor does a fire kindle in one's body. Who has seen the Baikunth Dhaam with his own eyes? Places of pilgrimage for the living are here, in this world. Nowhere else.

Night.

Ammi, asleep. Suddenly.

– What has happened to you people? Both of you are sleeping unmindful of me. Get up and attend to me.

The daughter bends close to her.

– Ammu, what's the matter?

– The crows are making such a lot of noise, caw-caw-caw ... I can't bear the sound of their beating wings. Drive them far away. Far away. Let me not hear them.

The daughter opens the window and makes noises as though driving away the crows. Then she closes the window and by way of reassuring her mother.

– Ammu, go to sleep now. All of them have flown away.

– Who all?

– The pigeons, Ammu.

– Were they pigeons?

– Yes.

– There must be a cat lurking outside to pounce on them.

– No, Ammu, there's nothing outside.

– You don't know, ladki. There is a lion crouching there. He will eat them up.

Susan spoons water into Ammu's mouth.

– Who has placed the earthen lamp under the tree? There is a wind blowing. It will be extinguished ... Cracks are appearing in my body. My limbs are falling apart.

Who is this man with a bright blue face? Has he come to fetch me?

Call my son quickly.

Come close to me, beta ... Bid me farewell.

Susan, why is it so dark? Don't remove the ladder from under my feet. I'll climb it myself ... You lazy thing, bring me my white shoes. I have to go up to Mashobra.

Ladki, ask your pitaji to wait for me.

I'm coming ...

Why are we going via Kali bari? They must be sacrificing goats and buffaloes there.

Away, away ... A copper–coloured maneater is after me. How can I slip past her? She'll lift me by her horns ...

Where are these clouds of darkness coming from? What are you rolling me up in? No! Don't touch my eyes. Ladki, call your brother. Call him quickly. He'll untether my horse for me. I'll ride it across the sea.

The daughter, touching her mother's hand.

– Ammu, dip deeply as you bathe. Everything will be all right.

A deep breath, a shudder and then, only silence.

Writer par excellence, **Krishna Sobti**'s contribution to Indian literature crosses the boundaries of culture. Her innovative use of language and technique and refreshing delineation of strong women characters opened new vistas in Hindi literature.

One of the most creative and engaging aspects of Krishna Sobti's writings is her lively language. Her contribution to Hindi is immense as she has added a multitude of new words and expressions to the language and has experimented with and successfully introduced new styles and techniques of writing. After her first novel, *Daar Se Bichhudi*, she went on to write several enthralling works like *Mitron Marjani*, *Surajmukhi Andhere Ke*, *Zindaginama*, *Ai Ladki*, *Hum Hashmat*, *Yaaron ke Yaar*, *Teen Pahad*, *Badalon Ke Ghere*, *Sobti Ek Sohbat*, and *Samay Sargam*, amongst others. Each of her works has an unusual use of the Hindi language, highly coloured with the flavour of the region the story is set in, for example, Punjab in *Daar Se Bichhudi*; Rajasthan in *Mitron Marjani*; and the suave Urdu-Hindi of the nawabs of Old Delhi in *Dil-O-Danish*.

Her writings revolve around Partition, upheaval and turmoil in Indian society, man-woman relationship, feudalism and dissolution of human values. Her works have been translated into Indian and foreign languages. *Ai Ladki* has been translated into Swedish, *Sobti Ek Sohbat* into Swedish and Urdu and *Mitron Marjani* into Russian.

She has received the Sahitya Akademi Award for her magnum opus, *Zindaginama*, the first woman writer to receive the award for Hindi. The First Katha Chudamani Award was conferred on her, in 1999, for Lifetime Literary Achievement. She is also the recipient of a number of other literary awards including the Hindi Academy Award, the Shiromani Award, Maithili Sharan Gupt Samman, Shalaka Samman and the Sadbhavna Puraskar besides a number of Fellowships including the exclusive Shimla and Punjab University Fellowships and the Sahitya Akademi Fellowship.

Krishna Sobti lives in Delhi and is currently working on two novels, *Gujarat se Gujarat* and *Hello Server*. She stays in our minds as a gutsy, indomitable woman who likes to live life on her own terms and who – as a writer and as an individual – has created a niche for herself in Hindi literature that is rightfully hers.

Shivanath is a Dogri scholar, writer and translator. He is a Retired Member of Post and Telegraph Board, the ex officio Additional Secretary to the Government of India. He has to his credit nine books relating to Dogri literature published by the Sahitya Akademi and two books published by the Dogri Samstha, Jammu. He was the editor of the first two issues of *Uttara*, a literary digest of six North indian languages and editor (Dogri) for the project Encyclopaedia of Indian Literature of the Sahitya Akademi. He was a member of the Dogri Advisory Board of the Sahitya Akademi as well as a member of the Executive Board of the Akademi.

Prokash Karmakar is one of India's most original and outstanding contemporary painters. He is able to blend and fuse Eastern and Western art and still stamp each painting with his unique creativity and individuality. His magnificent distortions offer a profound insight into his creative imagination and the experiences gained from his life as an orphan. He has exhibited in innumerable solo and group shows.

Delhi Art Gallery was started in 1993 with the works of a few contemporary artists. It now has one of the largest collections of Indian contemporary art in the world. The gallery recognizes the disparity in terms of prices and recognition between the old masters vis-a-vis the contemporary artists and is addressing the issue. They offer a significant number of works to all major auction houses and are planning a number of exhibitions abroad.

ABOUT KATHA

Katha, a registered nonprofit organization set up in September 1989, works in the areas of education, publishing and community development and endeavours to spread the joy of reading, knowing and living amongst adults and children. Our main objective is **to enhance the pleasures of reading for children and adults**, for experienced readers as well as for those who are just beginning to read. Our attempt is also to stimulate an interest in lifelong learning that will help the child grow into a confident, self-reliant, responsible and responsive adult, as also to help break down gender, cultural and social stereotypes, encourage and foster excellence, applaud quality literature and translations in and between the various Indian languages and work towards community revitalization and economic resurgence. The two wings of Katha are **Katha Vilasam** and **Kalpavriksham**

KATHA VILASAM, the Story Research and Resource Centre, was set up to foster and applaud quality Indian literature and take these to a wider audience through quality translations and related activities like **Katha Books, Academic Publishing**, the **Katha Awards** for fiction, translation and editing, **Kathakaar** – the Centre for Children's Literature, **Katha Barani** – the Translation Resource Centre, the **Katha Translation Exchange Programme**, **Translation Contests**. **Kanchi** – the Katha National Institute of Translation promotes translation through **Katha Academic Centres** in various Indian universities, **Faculty Enhancement Programmes** through Workshops, seminars and discussions, **Sishya** – Katha Clubs in colleges, **Storytellers Unlimited** – the art and craft of storytelling and **KathaRasa** – performances, art fusion and other events at the Katha Centre.

KALPAVRIKSHAM, the Centre for Sustainable Learning, was set up to foster quality education that is relevant and fun for children from nonliterate families, and to promote community revitalization and economic resurgence work. These goals crystallized in the development of the following areas of activities. **Katha Khazana** which includes **Katha Student Support Centre, Katha Public School**, **Katha School of Entrepreneurship, KITES** – the Katha Information Technology and eCommerce School, **Iccha Ghar – The Intel Computer Clubhouse @ Katha, Hamara Gaon** and **The Mandals** – Maa, Bapu, Balika, Balak and Danadini, **Shakti Khazana** was set up for skills upgradation and income generation activities comprising the Khazana Coop. **Kalpana Vilasam** is the cell for regular research and development of teaching/learning materials, curricula, syllabi, content comprising **Teacher Training, TaQeEd — The Teachers Alliance for Quality eEducation. Tamasha's World!** comprises **Tamasha! the Children's magazine,** ***Dhammakdhum! www.tamasha.org*** **and ANU – Animals, Nature and YOU!**